Illustrated by
María Cristina Brusca

Henry Holt and Company · New York

María Cristina Brusca · Tona Wilson

❧ The COOK ❧
and the KING

Higham up in the mountains of South America there was once a tiny kingdom ruled by an unfair and bossy king.

The people of this kingdom worked very hard. But once a year, at the end of summer, they stopped and thanked their *Pachamama*, Mother Earth, for giving them life. They put aside their work for a few days and celebrated with a carnival. They danced in the streets and played with their friends, splashing them with cool water. And they picked flowering basil, waved it in the air, and tickled each other's noses with it as they danced. So throughout the year the sweet smell of basil always reminded them of the joy of carnival and of their friends.

But the king did not celebrate carnival. He watched the revelers from his stone turret, for he felt that fun, like work, was beneath his station. He had even forgotten how to dance.

Next door to the king lived a young cook named Florinda. She was famous throughout the land for her *empanadas*, little meat pies, which she baked and sold at market. And she had the most beautiful basil plant in the kingdom. At carnival time, people came from far and wide to ask her for a sprig of basil. Even the king, standing on his stone turret, would sniff the delicious smells that came from Florinda's clay oven. But he never spoke to her.

ne day, when Florinda was lighting her clay oven, she saw the palace cook slam the heavy doors and stomp off with all her cookware in tow. The king came out onto his turret and barked down to Florinda: "You there! Come cook for me! Immediately!"

Florinda looked up from her work and asked, "And what will you pay me if I do?" The king named a salary that was twice what Florinda could make selling *empanadas*.

"I don't know," said Florinda, who was just as stubborn as the king was. "I'll have to think about it." And she went into her kitchen. Soon the smell of frying onions came teasingly to the king's nostrils.

The king paced the turret hungrily. Finally he called out to Florinda and offered her even more money.

"Well, I suppose I might. . . ." she said. Remembering the cook's stormy departure, she added quickly, "But you'll have to promise not to fire me."

The king looked at her, shocked. "I'll promise you nothing of the kind!" he answered haughtily.

"Then I won't cook for you," replied Florinda.

But the king was dreaming of an endless supply of the best *empanadas* in the world.

"Well . . ." added Florinda, "if you won't promise not to fire me, then at least grant me one wish, one time, whenever I ask—plus that salary you mentioned!"

"Oh, all right," said the king, overcome by his empty stomach. "But remember—you're just a cook! No sticking your nose into the serious business of the kingdom!"

"And isn't food serious business?" replied Florinda.

That day Florinda went to work for the king. He was pleased with her cooking. But soon she noticed that he was very bad tempered on the days when he had to settle disputes between his subjects. Since he had spent most of his life in a palace and didn't understand his people's problems, the king's judgments were hasty, foolish, and unfair. And instead of admitting that he was wrong, he sulked, or kicked his throne, or complained about everything, especially Florinda's cooking.

One day Carmen Vásquez and her neighbor Teresa came to the king with a dispute.

Carmen said she had been waiting patiently for her peaches to ripen. She explained that one night she had gone to bed early, planning to pick them in the morning and take them to market to sell.

But when she woke up, there was not a single peach left on her tree. She ran out to the gate just in time to see Teresa hurrying toward the market with a basket on her head.

Carmen ran after her, but by the time she caught up, Teresa had sold all the peaches. Carmen asked Teresa to give her her fruit back, but of course that was impossible. Then she asked for the money, but Teresa claimed the peaches had been her own.

Carmen took the king to her tree, so he could see for himself. "Look!" she said. "You can even see where that thief picked my peaches!"

"Who are you calling a thief?" retorted Teresa, shaking her fist at Carmen. "I have a tree too, you know," she added. "Come see it for yourself, Your Majesty." And she led him to her house, and pointed to a beautiful, healthy . . . *walnut tree*!

"That's not a peach tree!" shouted Carmen.

The king covered his ears with his hands. He wanted to get home to his comfortable palace. "Who cares about these silly women and their peaches?" he thought. He looked at the walnut tree and at the peach tree. "Both of you have trees. Teresa keeps the money," he said hastily. "Case dismissed." And he hurried home with his hands over his ears.

Carmen was furious about this judgment, and the next day she told Florinda about it when they met at market. "Hmmm!" said Florinda. "What kind of decision is that? That boss of mine needs a good lesson." So she bought some turnips and went home.

That night she served the king a big plate of mashed turnips. "TURNIPS!" said the king, who had been looking forward to one of Florinda's tasty dinners. "You know I HATE turnips! Where did these awful things come from?"

"Why, I got them from my potato plant just this morning," said Florinda.

"What?" shouted the king. "Who ever heard of turnips growing on a potato plant?"

"Well," said Florinda, "I suppose it *is* unusual. But after all, you yourself said that peaches can grow on a walnut tree, so I guess anything's possible."

The king turned as red as a beet. "Didn't I tell you not to stick your nose into my business?" he shouted. And he stomped up to bed without any supper.

i t was not long before two more people, doña Paula and don José, came to the king with a problem.

One day doña Paula had come to town with her mare and its new little foal. While she was doing some business at the market, don José had led the little foal away. When doña Paula tried to get it back, don José claimed that it was *his* foal and that his lame old stallion was its mother!

The king ordered them to bring all the horses together in front of his palace. He made the mare stand on one side of the yard and the stallion on the other. Then he led the foal to the middle. He declared pompously that the first horse the foal went toward would be deemed its mother. The shaky little foal tottered in the direction of don José's horse, and the king declared the stallion its mother and awarded the foal to don José.

Florinda shook her head. "What kind of foolish decision is that?" she muttered to herself.

That evening the king was sitting in the kitchen watching Florinda shell peas. "Look!" she said suddenly. "There go don Pascual and his mother!"

The king looked out the window, but all he could see was two old men, one walking with a limp a few steps behind his friend. "But that's don Pascual and don Cristóbal!" said the king. "Nobody's mother is there at all!"

"Well," said Florinda. "I have to admit that don Cristóbal is a strange mother, but don Pascual is following him, isn't he?"

"So what?" said the king.

"Well, didn't you yourself say the stallion was the foal's mother because the foal followed him? If that old stallion can be a mother, then so can don Cristóbal!"

"How dare you?" roared the king, leaping up from the table and brandishing a kitchen knife. "Not one more word out of you, Cook, or you'll be in big trouble!" And he stomped up to bed without any supper.

efore long two more villagers came to the king with a problem. They had made a bet with each other: Víctor, a poor shepherd, had boasted that he could stay out in the desert all night with only his poncho to keep him warm, and Elfidio, a rich merchant, had bet him fifty pesos that he could not. So that night Víctor had gone out to the desert with only his poncho, and in the morning he had returned, chilly but alive. The merchant said he must have warmed himself somehow and refused to pay the bet. Now they asked the king who should pay.

The king scowled at the shepherd and said, "If you were really out in the desert, tell me what you saw."

"I saw an owl, and I saw an opossum, and far, far away, up in the mountains, I saw a tiny little fire burning."

"Aha!" said the king. "You saw a fire, and that kept you warm!" And he ordered the shepherd to pay fifty pesos to the merchant.

Florinda, who was chopping onions in the kitchen, overheard the whole conversation. "That's so unfair," she thought, and she wept into the onions. That evening she kept perfectly quiet and didn't say a word about the case.

But the next morning, when the king came downstairs for his breakfast, he saw that while the fire was roaring in the fireplace, the frying pan was over by the door.

"Those eggs are *never* going to fry!" he shouted. "What on earth are you thinking of?"

"Oh," said Florinda, "I was just thinking of your own wise words. If a man can warm himself by a tiny little fire way up in the mountains, then why can't the eggs fry over here when there is a roaring fire just across the room?"

"I'll show you a roaring fire!" said the king, and he stomped out of the kitchen without any breakfast.

The king ordered his men to build a huge fire outside the palace. Turning to Florinda, he screamed, "You shall burn for sticking your nose into the serious business of the kingdom!"

"Very well," she answered calmly. "We all must go sometime."

When the fire was good and hot, the executioner led her to the flames. Just as he was about to throw her in, she called out to the king, "Oh, King, don't you remember you promised to grant me one little wish?"

"Go ahead, what is it?" growled the king.

"Come closer, so I can whisper it in your ear," she said.

Florinda whispered, "All I ask is that you close your eyes." When his eyes were shut, Florinda took a sprig of fresh basil from her apron pocket and brushed it across the king's face.

The smell of the basil startled the king. He sniffed, and thought of carnival time. He sniffed again, and thought of himself, apart, on his stone turret, high above the carnival. He sniffed once more and remembered suddenly a time before he was king, when he too had danced and laughed and waved a sprig of basil. He had had friends then, and they had tickled his face, and he had laughed. A faint smile broke out on the king's face. It grew, and grew . . .

Then the king opened his eyes and saw the roaring flames and the people looking at him with fear and anger. He saw no joy and laughter. No one would ever dare to tickle his nose with basil now—except for Florinda. And *she* was about to be burned!

"Stop!" he shouted to the executioner. He grabbed Florinda's hand and pulled her away from the fire. He looked at the people and did the bravest thing he'd ever done in his life. "I've made a mistake," he said. "And I'm sorry."

The king sent for Carmen and her neighbor Teresa, don José and doña Paula, Víctor the shepherd and Elfidio the merchant. "I've been hasty, and foolish, and unfair," he said.

He told Teresa to give Carmen the money she'd gotten for her peaches.

And he told don José to return doña Paula's foal.

Then he told the merchant to give the shepherd what was rightfully due to him and advised them both not to make any more foolish bets.

And then the king made the wisest decision of all: He named
Florinda the Official Judge of the Kingdom.

He offered her a room at the palace, but she preferred to return
to her cottage and her basil plant. Florinda became known far and
wide as the fairest judge in all the land. And the basil leaf became
the symbol of justice in that kingdom.

As for the king, he was busy cooking! Florinda taught him all her culinary wisdom, and with time he became an excellent—if a bit eccentric—cook. Sometimes, when he was not sure a recipe he'd invented was *really* good (like the time he made a pie out of sausages, whipped cream, and basil, his favorite herb), he invited Florinda over to the palace to taste it. For he knew that *she* at least would always tell him exactly what she thought.

Authors' Note

The Cook and the King was inspired by a South American folktale. Although there were not really kings in the mountains of South America, there were viceroys, who ruled by proxy for the king of Spain. The clothes worn by the king in this book are based on those of the kings depicted on Spanish playing cards.

The indigenous peoples of the Andean countries have traditionally thanked the *Pachamama* (Quechua word for Mother Earth) for each year's harvest, which takes place in late summer. A time for giving thanks and forgetting one's troubles, celebrations of *Pachamama* now coincide with the European carnival.

Customs at carnival time vary, but in the Calchaquí valleys in northwestern Argentina, people do pick basil, which flowers at the end of summer. They carry sprigs of it and wave them about as they dance. They also splash each other with water and play with flour, the way people do with shaving cream on Halloween here. In some places, cornstalks are carried, and some people wear costumes or dress their horses with willow branches.

Everywhere, there is music. Some of the instruments traditionally used in the northwest of Argentina are the *charango,* a small stringed instrument made with the shell of an armadillo, the *bombo* and the *caja,* different kinds of drums, the *quena,* a flute, the *sikuri* or panpipes, and the *erque,* a very long horn.

To Luis María Torres Agüero, Ujshpa, Malanzán　　—M.C.B.

To Ana Jimena Martínez Lignelli　　—T.W.

Text copyright © 1993 by María Cristina Brusca and Tona Wilson / Illustrations copyright © 1993 by María Cristina Brusca
All rights reserved, including the right to reproduce this book or portions thereof in any form.
Published by Henry Holt and Company, Inc., 115 West 18th Street, New York, New York 10011.
Published simultaneously in Canada by Fitzhenry & Whiteside Ltd., 91 Granton Drive, Richmond Hill, Ontario L4B 2N5.

Library of Congress Cataloging-in-Publication Data
Brusca, María Cristina / The cook and the king / María Cristina Brusca, Tona Wilson; illustrated by María Cristina Brusca.
Summary: High in the mountains of South America, a wise cook teaches a stubborn, bossy king how to rule his kingdom wisely.
ISBN 0-8050-2355-0 (alk. paper) [1. Folklore—South America.　2. Kings, queens, rulers, etc.—Folklore.]　I. Wilson, Tona.　II. Title.
PZ8.1.B8374Co　1993　　398.2—dc20　[E]　92-25812　　Printed in the United States of America on acid-free paper. ∞

1　3　5　7　9　10　8　6　4　2

First edition